BLACKBEARD'S SWORD

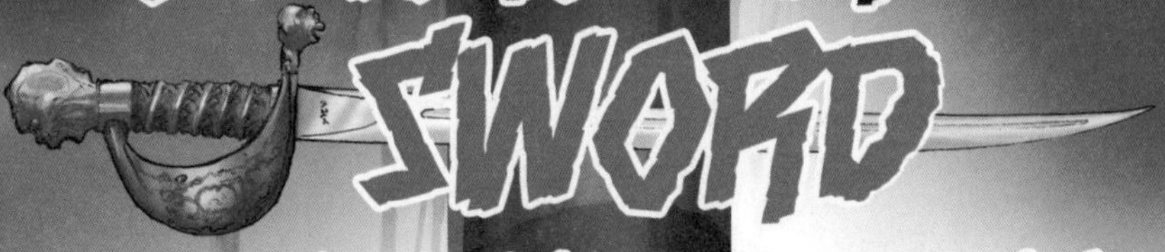

THE PIRATE KING OF THE CAROLINAS

by Liam O'Donnell   illustrated by Mike Spoor

Librarian Reviewer
Laurie K. Holland
Media Specialist (National Board Certified), Edina, MN
MA in Elementary Education, Minnesota State University, Mankato

Reading Consultant
Elizabeth Stedem
Educator/Consultant, Colorado Springs, CO
MA in Elementary Education, University of Denver, CO

STONE ARCH BOOKS
Minneapolis   San Diego

Graphic Flashbacks are published by Stone Arch Books,
151 Good Counsel Drive, P.O. Box 669,
Mankato, Minnesota 56002.
www.stonearchbooks.com

Library of Congress Cataloging-in-Publication Data
O'Donnell, Liam, 1970–
Blackbeard's Sword: The Pirate King of the Carolinas / by Liam O'Donnell; illustrated by Mike Spoor.
p. cm. — (Graphic Flash)
ISBN-13: 978-159889-309-0 (library binding)
ISBN-10: 1-59889-309-2 (library binding)
ISBN-13: 978-159889-404-2 (paperback)
ISBN-10: 1-59889-404-8 (paperback)
1. Graphic Novels. 2. Teach, Edward, 1718– —Comic books, strips, etc.
I. Spoor, Mike.
PN6727.O35 B53 2007
741.5'973—dc22 2006028030

Summary: Edward Teach, known far and wide as Blackbeard, holds the coast of North and South Carolina in a grip of terror. Lieutenant Maynard and his men of the Royal Navy decide to capture the pirate, but they need help piloting their way through the shallow maze of coves and inlets. They enlist the aid of local fishermen Jacob Webster and his father, but Maynard doesn't count on the fact that Jacob may be leading them into trouble. The boy thinks Blackbeard is a hero!

Art Director: Heather Kindseth
Graphic Designer: Brann Garvey

1 2 3 4 5 6 11 10 09 08 07 06

Printed in the United States of America.

TABLE OF CONTENTS

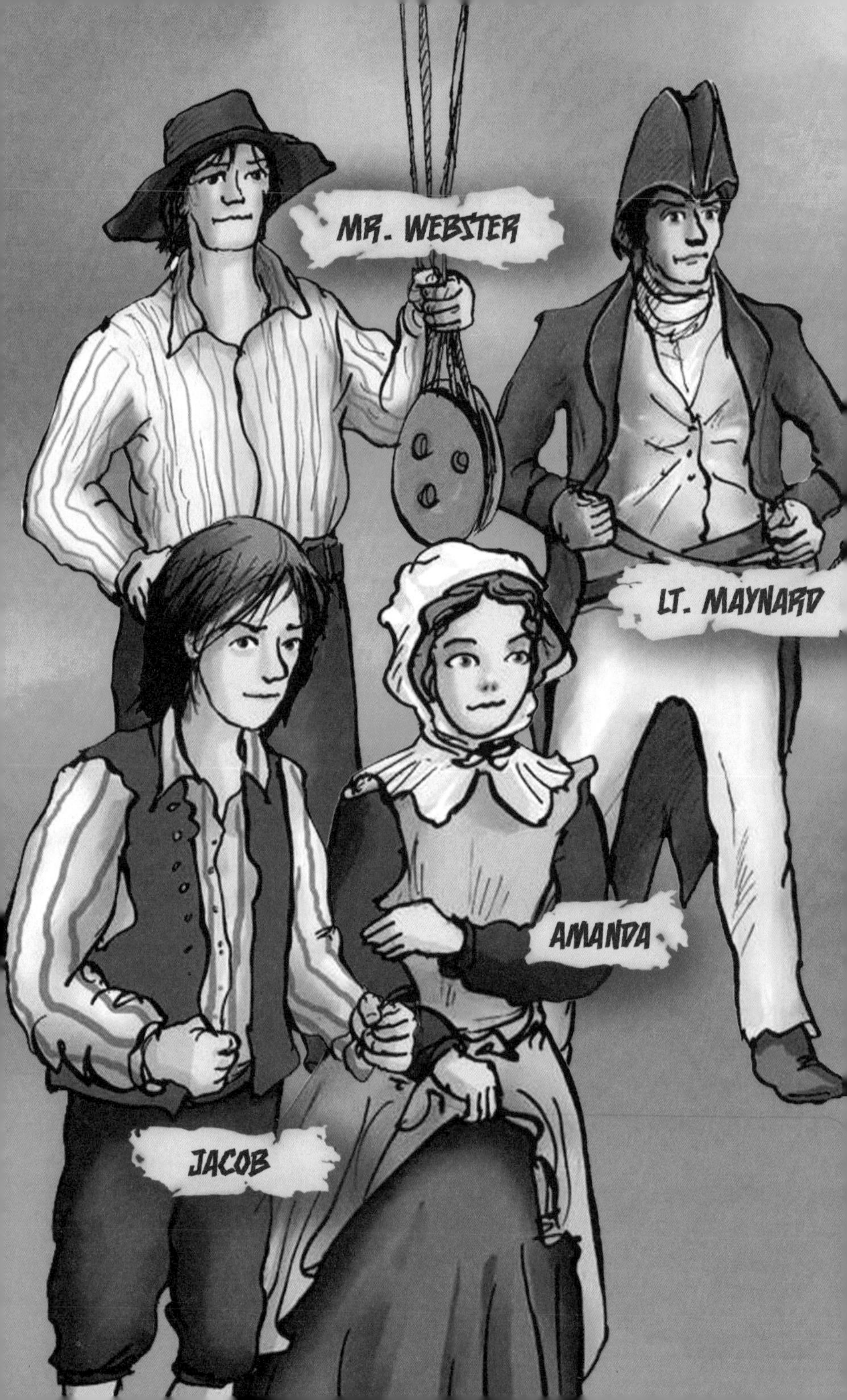
MR. WEBSTER
LT. MAYNARD
AMANDA
JACOB

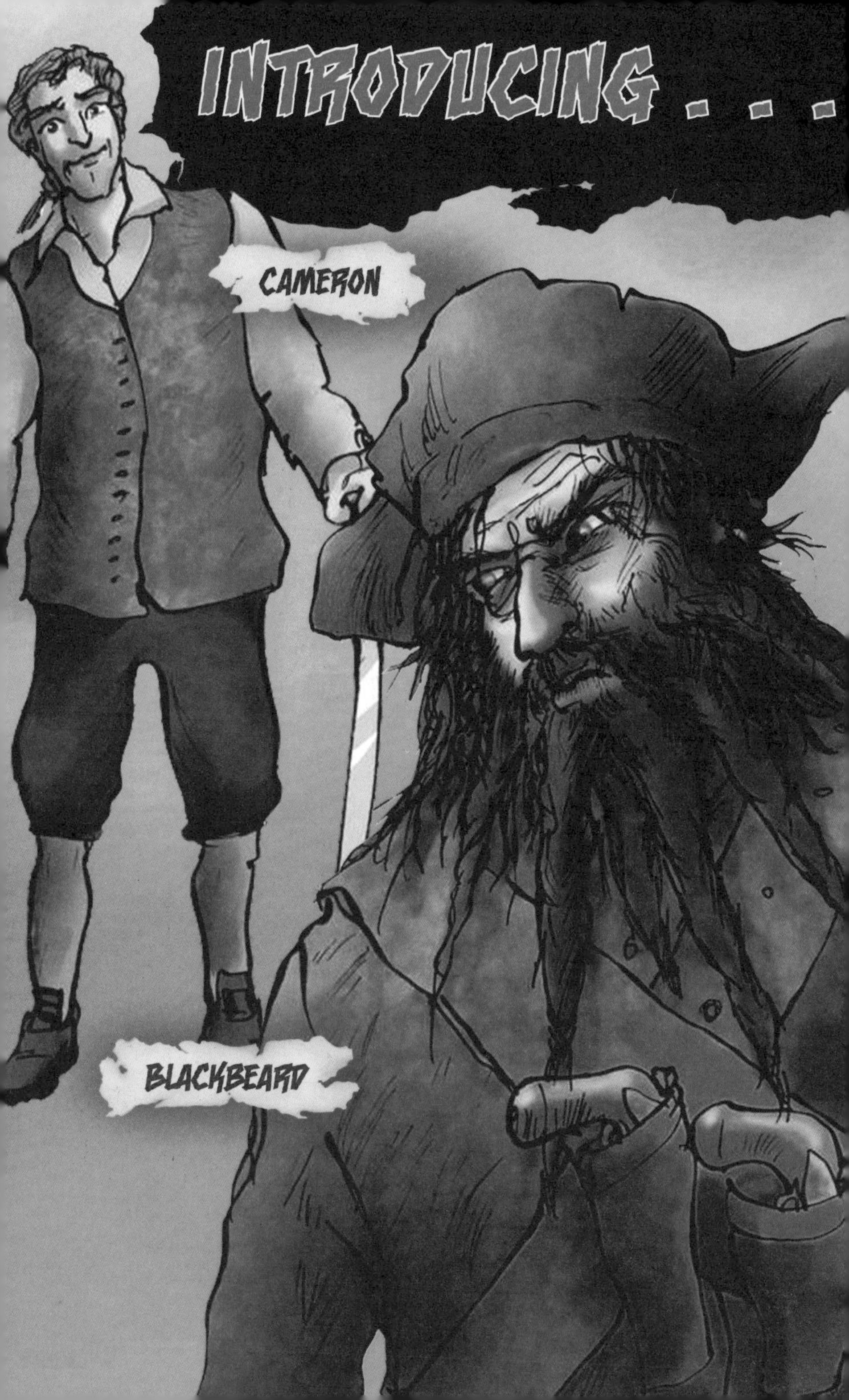
INTRODUCING . . .
CAMERON
BLACKBEARD

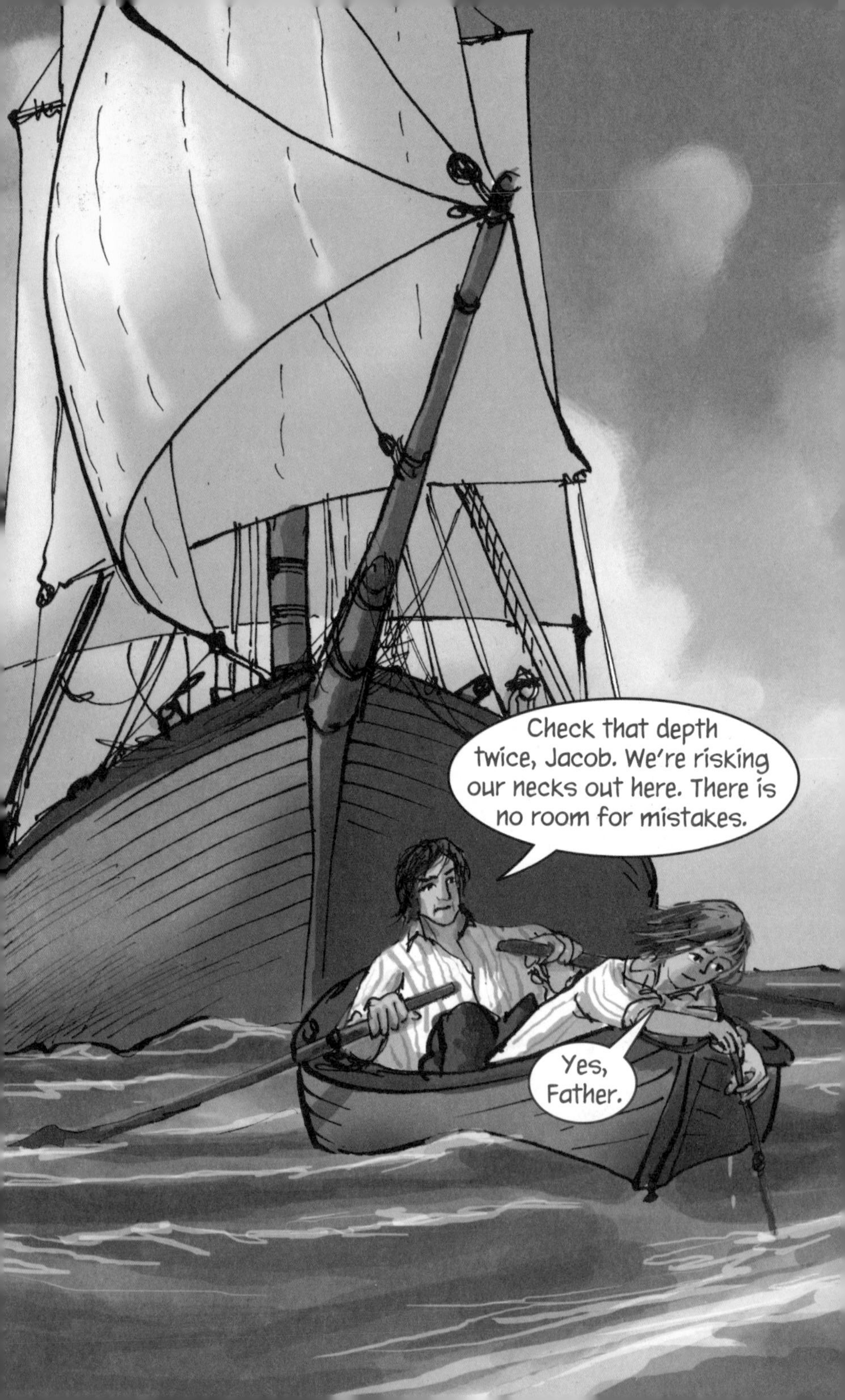
Check that depth twice, Jacob. We're risking our necks out here. There is no room for mistakes.
Yes, Father.

Chapter 1

PIRATE HUNTERS' MISTAKE

It was a cold November afternoon when I tried to save the life of Blackbeard the pirate. The year was 1718. I was helping my father guide a ship called the *Jane* through the shallow waters of the Pamlico Sound. Blackbeard's ship, the *Adventure*, was anchored in this inlet, and we were on the hunt for him.

"What's our depth?" my father asked for the millionth time that hour. We were checking for sandbars beneath the water. Lieutenant Maynard and his ship, the *Jane*, were following us. Maynard's pirate hunters depended on us to find a path for the ship through the shallow water.

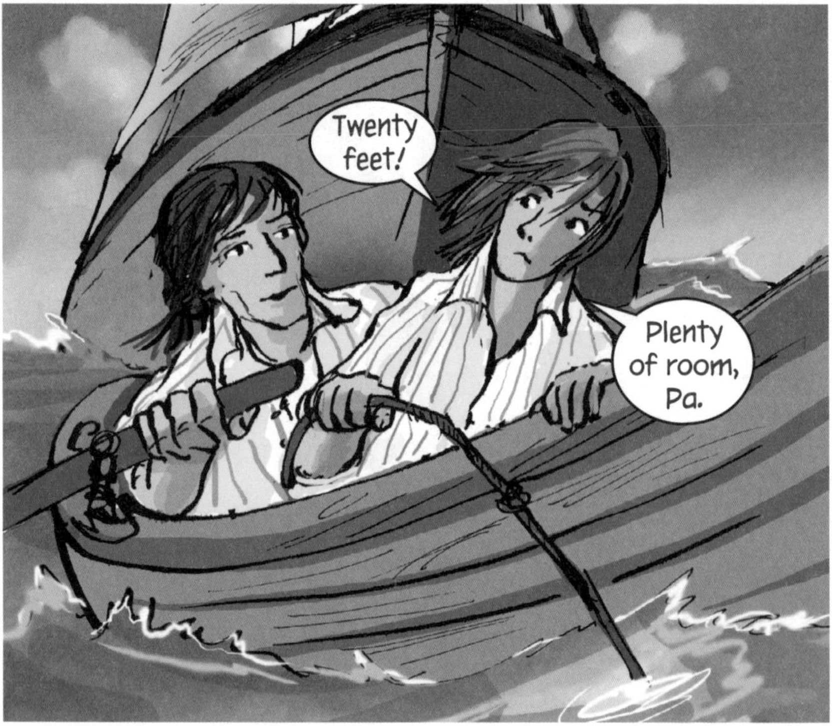
Twenty feet!
Plenty of room, Pa.

That was a lie. The water was shallow here and the plumb line told me so. Ten feet below these waters was a sandbank that would stop the *Jane* and maybe save the life of my hero, Blackbeard the pirate.

My father signalled the *Jane* to let them know that the water was deep enough. The *Jane* moved forward into the shallow water. I braced myself for what was coming next.

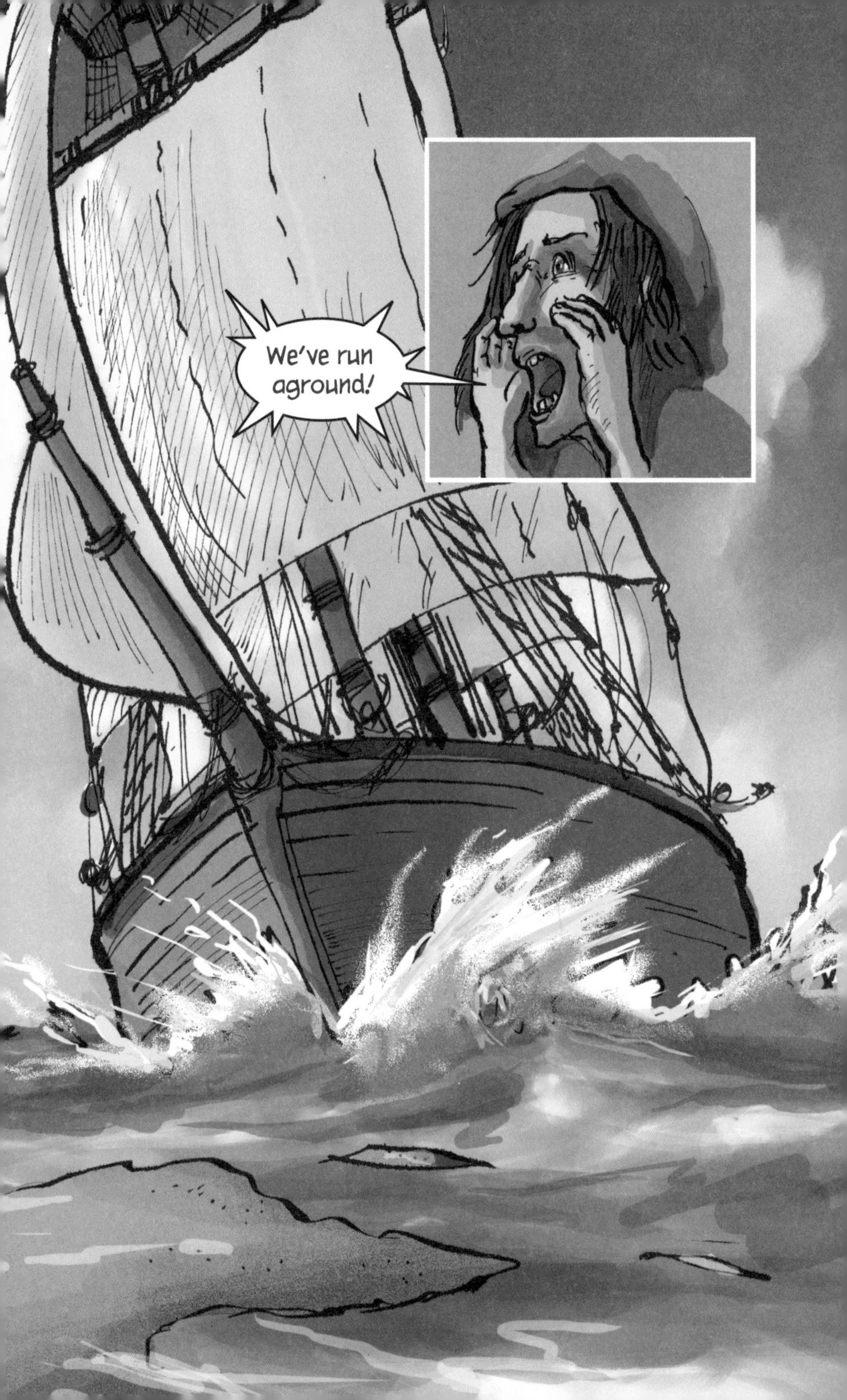
We've run aground!

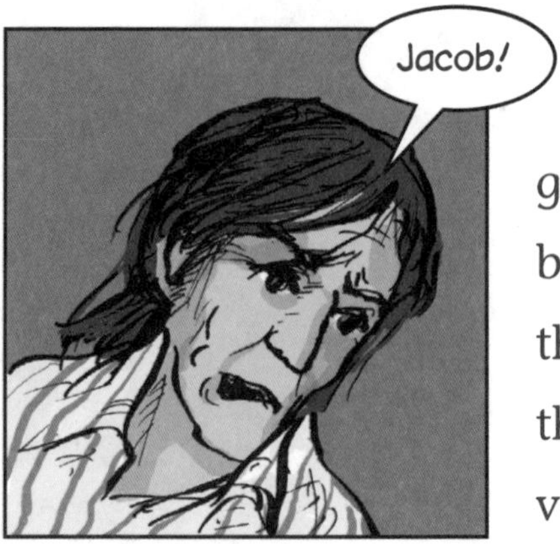
Jacob!

My father groaned. My betrayal hung in the air, and I knew that I had made a very big mistake.

With the *Jane* trapped on a sandbank, Blackbeard could now escape Lieutenant Maynard and his men. But Blackbeard didn't run. The low tide and hidden sandbanks had grabbed the hull of his ship and he was stuck too.

Our tiny pilot boat bobbed on the water only a few hundred yards away from Blackbeard's ship, the *Adventure*. The ship might have been stuck, but the cannons were working. Before we could get away, the gunports on the side of the *Adventure* opened. Black cannons pushed through the holes and pointed toward us.

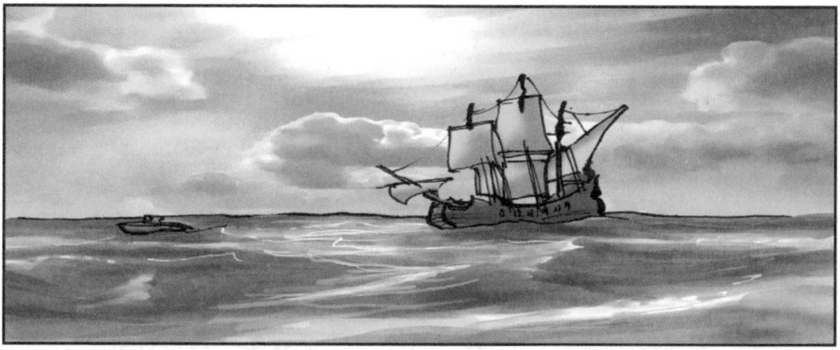

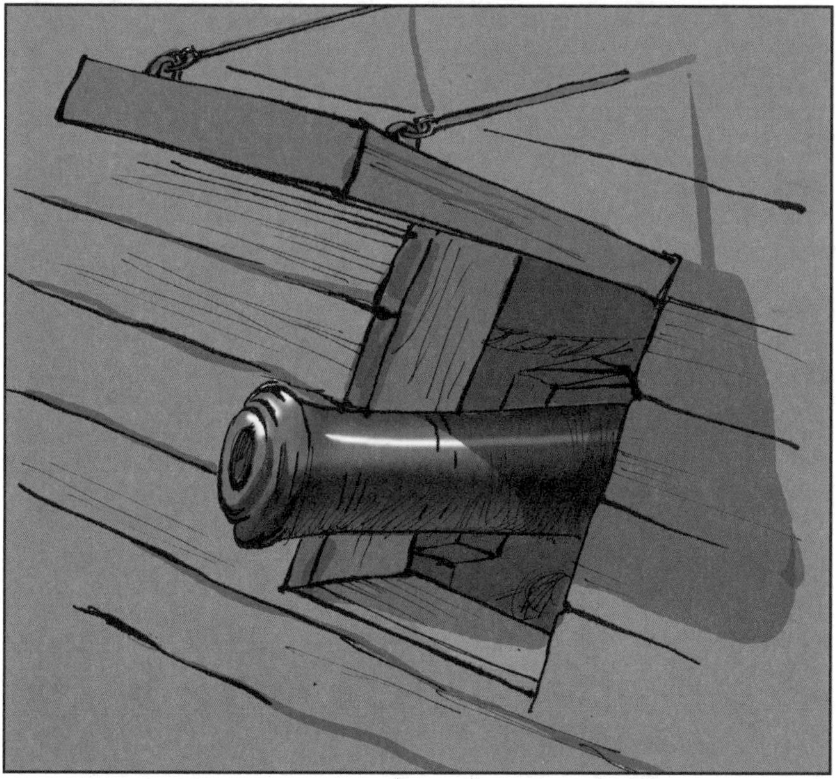

I had just saved Blackbeard, and now he was going to kill me. This wasn't how it was meant to go at all.

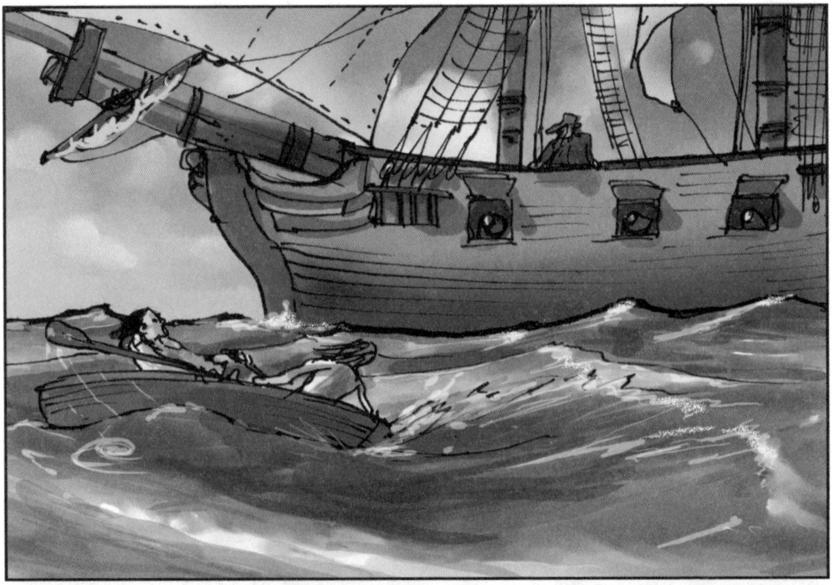

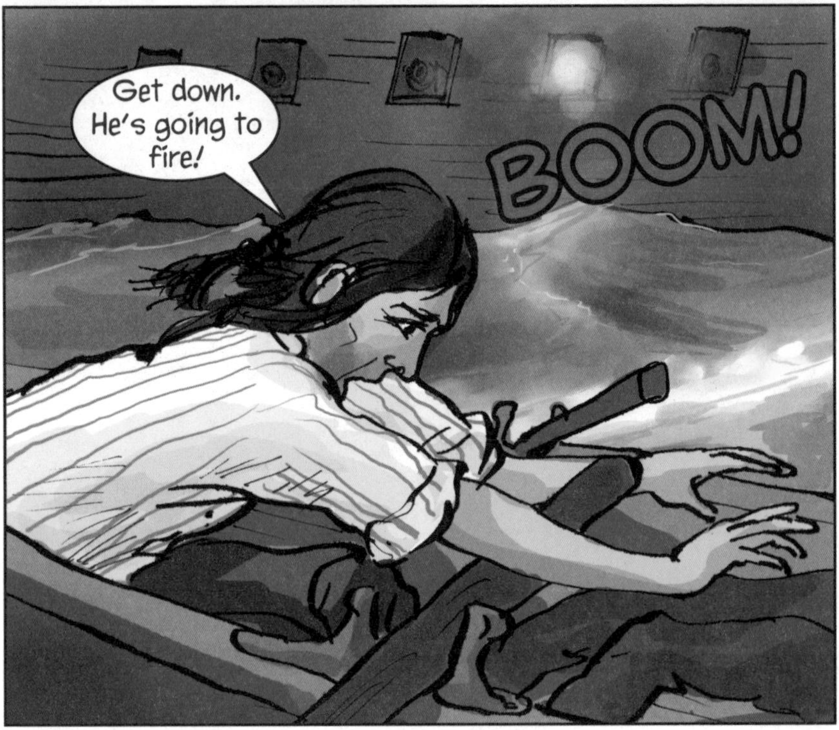
Get down. He's going to fire!
BOOM!

Chapter 2

PIRATE TALES

Before I can tell you what happened after Blackbeard blasted his cannons, let me tell you why I wanted to save the most wanted pirate sailing the high seas.

It's hard to believe some of the stories people tell about Blackbeard.

They say he stands as tall as a tree and as wide as a herring barrel. He wears an arsenal of knives and swords and pistols.

He has fourteen wives and fifty children, and people call him the King of Pirates.

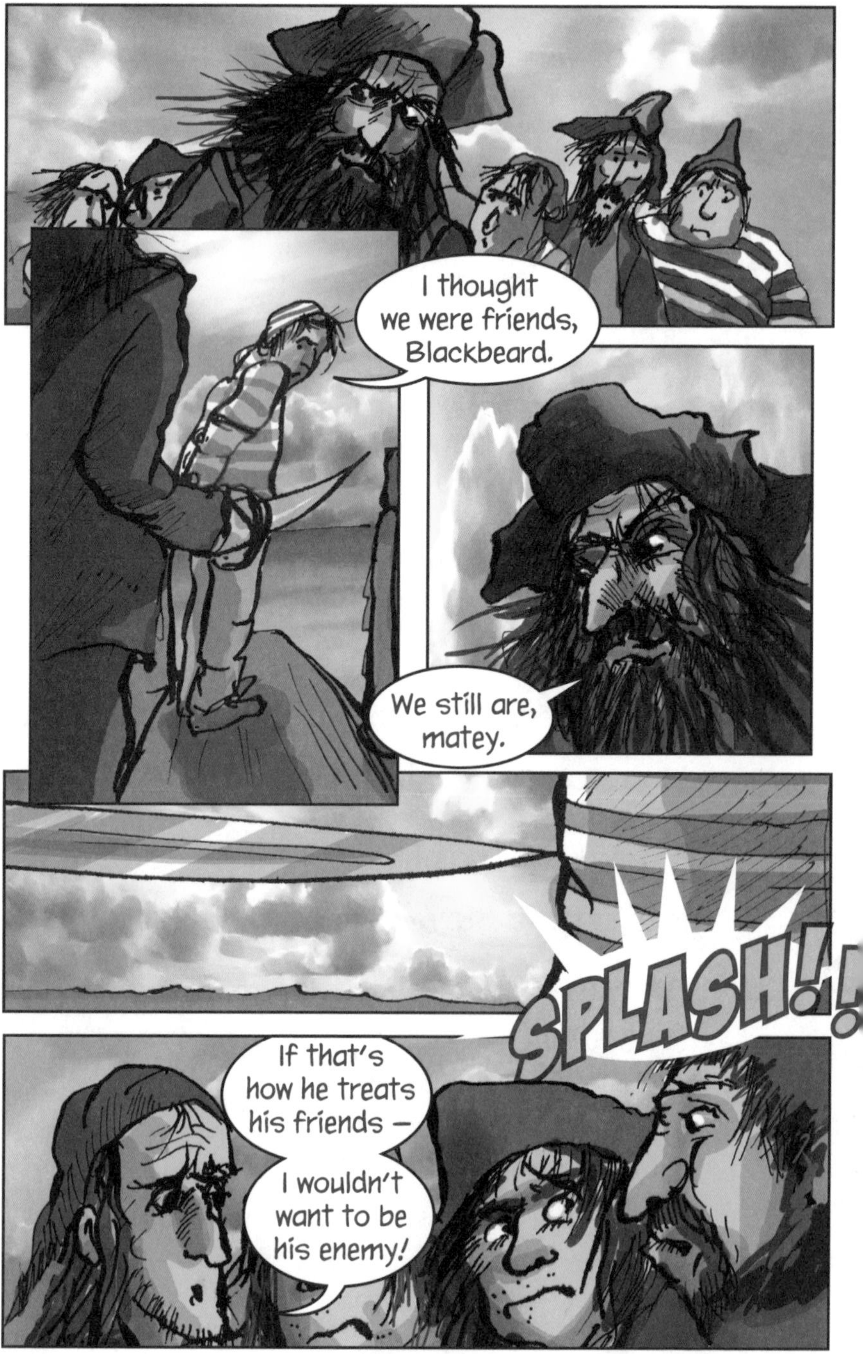
I thought we were friends, Blackbeard.
We still are, matey.
SPLASH!!
If that's how he treats his friends –
I wouldn't want to be his enemy!

At least that's the story I have heard. Who knows if it's true, but Blackbeard himself is real enough.

His real name is Edward Teach or Thatch. No one is certain. Anyone who was foolish enough to ask him is probably lying on the bottom of some ocean, turned into a feast for the eels.

He was born in England. In fact, he named his first ship *Queen Anne's Revenge*, after the queen of England herself. I wonder if anyone has told her about it.

Blackbeard's a good man, too, in my opinion. Once he held the entire city of Charleston hostage for a good purpose. His pirate fleet blockaded the city's harbor. Then Blackbeard appeared on his ship and demanded ransom from the city. But what did he ask for? Not gold, or fine silver, or a chest full of gems.

No, he wanted a doctor for his crew members who were sick. So, you can see that Blackbeard isn't always cruel and bloodthirsty. He is concerned for the health of his men.

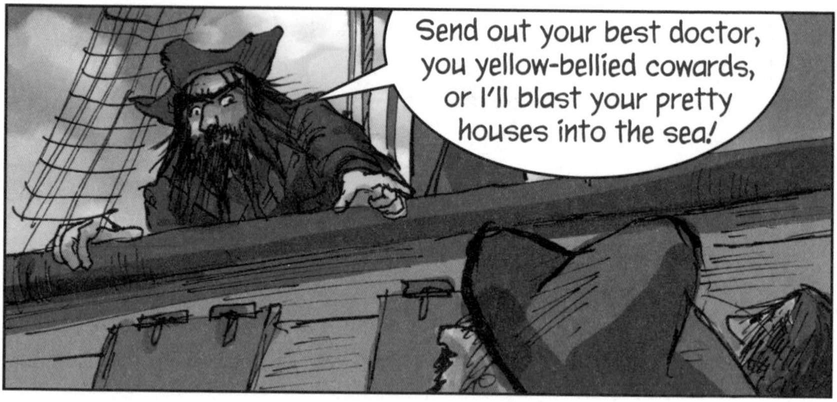
Send out your best doctor, you yellow-bellied cowards, or I'll blast your pretty houses into the sea!

My father and I have a difference of opinion about the matter.

"See?" I once told him. "Blackbeard is a good man. He takes care of his men."

"He is a selfish scoundrel," said my father. "If those pirates didn't spend their days drinking and cutting up one another with swords, they wouldn't need a doctor."

The city of Charleston did give in to Blackbeard's request. They had to. If they hadn't, Blackbeard would have pounded the city with his ship's forty cannons. Or he would have unleashed his crew of 300 fierce and powerful fighting men.

A doctor rowed out in a small boat and tended to his crew.

Chapter 3
A PLAN IS HATCHED

A few weeks ago, Blackbeard and his crew landed in my hometown to sell their treasure and buy supplies for their next voyage.

See, Amanda.

I told you Blackbeard was here. Isn't he the greatest?

If you like bullies and madmen.

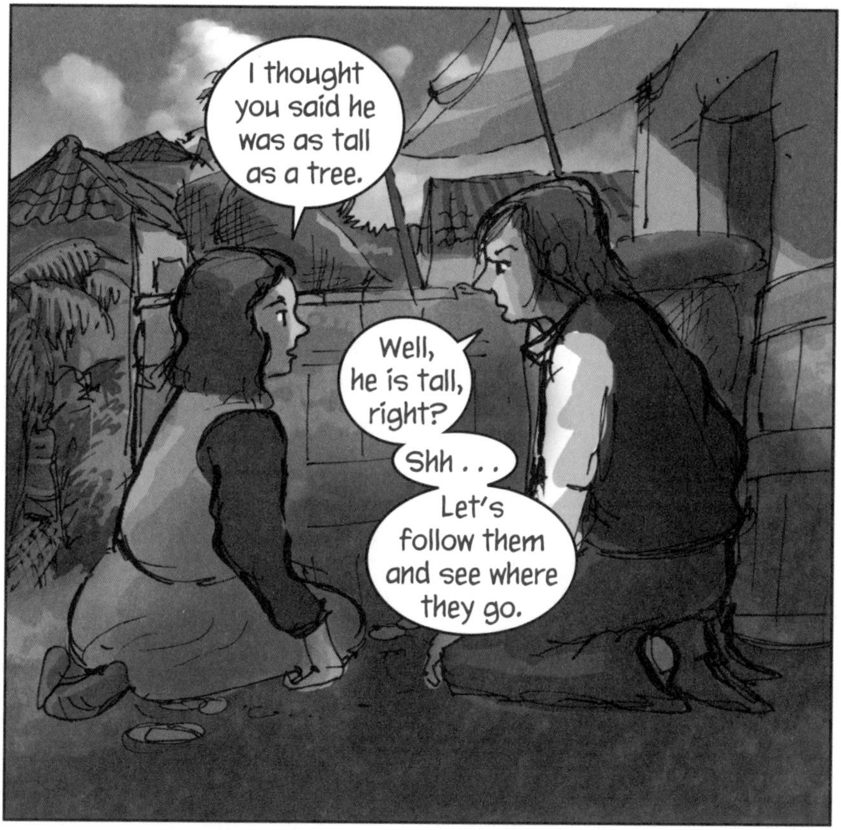
I thought you said he was as tall as a tree.
Well, he is tall, right?
Shh . . .
Let's follow them and see where they go.

"I don't know why you think pirates are so great, Jacob Webster," Amanda whispered from our hiding spot behind a stack of lobster traps.

"Pirates are free to go where they want and do what they please," I replied. "They don't stay in just one town. They sail around the world in search of treasure."

Amanda's father was a harbor pilot, just like my dad. They used their boats to guide large ships through the shallow waters of Pamlico Sound. With miles and miles of ocean out there, I couldn't understand how our fathers could be happy sailing the tiny waters around our harbor.

Last summer, Amanda and I played pirates every day. Now, all she wanted to play is school or some other boring game. Just like everyone else in Bathtown, Amanda was tired of pirates and their yelling, drinking, and rough ways.

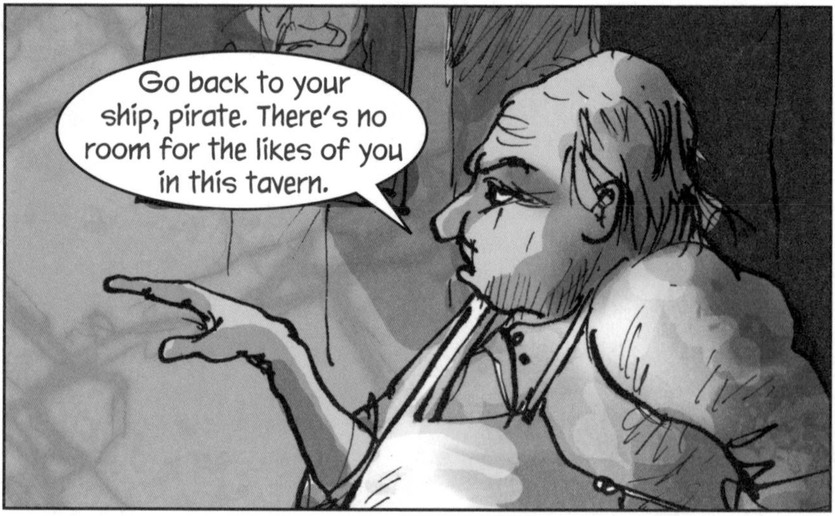
Go back to your ship, pirate. There's no room for the likes of you in this tavern.

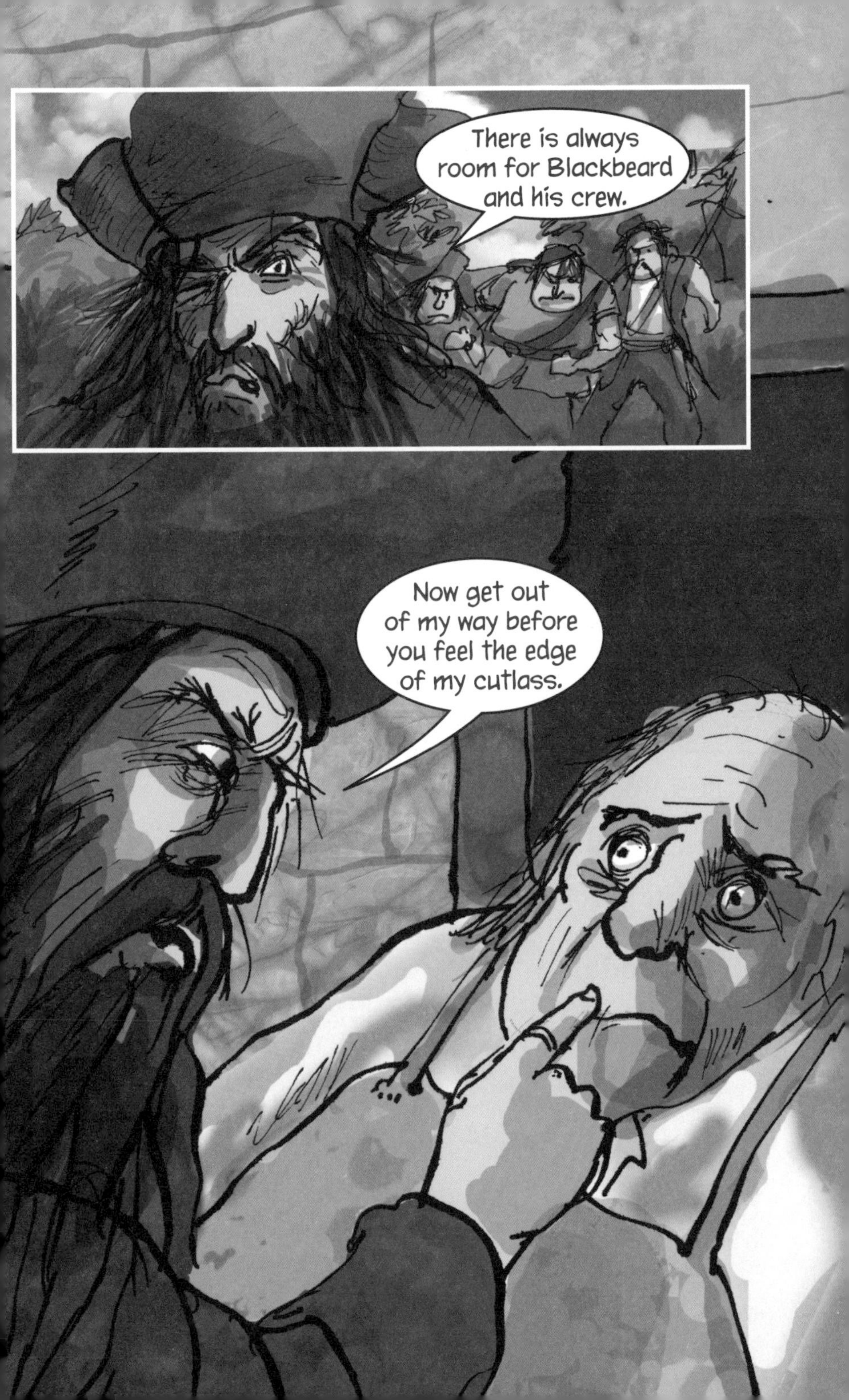
There is always room for Blackbeard and his crew.
Now get out of my way before you feel the edge of my cutlass.

"My father says there is a group of pirate hunters in town. They are going to capture Blackbeard," Amanda said after we left the tavern. She had chores to do back home and I struggled to keep up with her quick steps. "They were talking to your father this morning. He is going to lead them to Blackbeard's ship."

"He never said anything to me," I said. We arrived at the end of her street.

"Why would he?" she called over her shoulder as she ran along the cobblestones to her small house. "You would probably try to warn Blackbeard!"

I said nothing to my father about Blackbeard or pirate hunters when I got home. That night, Amanda's words ran through my mind. Early the next morning, I had a plan and made my move.

By the time Father found me hidden under the sails of his boat, it was too late to turn back. We were in the middle of the water with the *Jane* close behind.

This is no trip for a boy.

But I suppose it will do you good to see the end of that vile pirate.

I said nothing. How could I tell my father I was not on board to hunt pirates? I was there to warn Blackbeard the pirate and save his life.

Chapter 4

BLACKBEARD'S TRUE COLORS

So, to get back to my story, there we were early that morning, with both the *Jane* and the *Adventure* stuck on the sandbars, when . . .

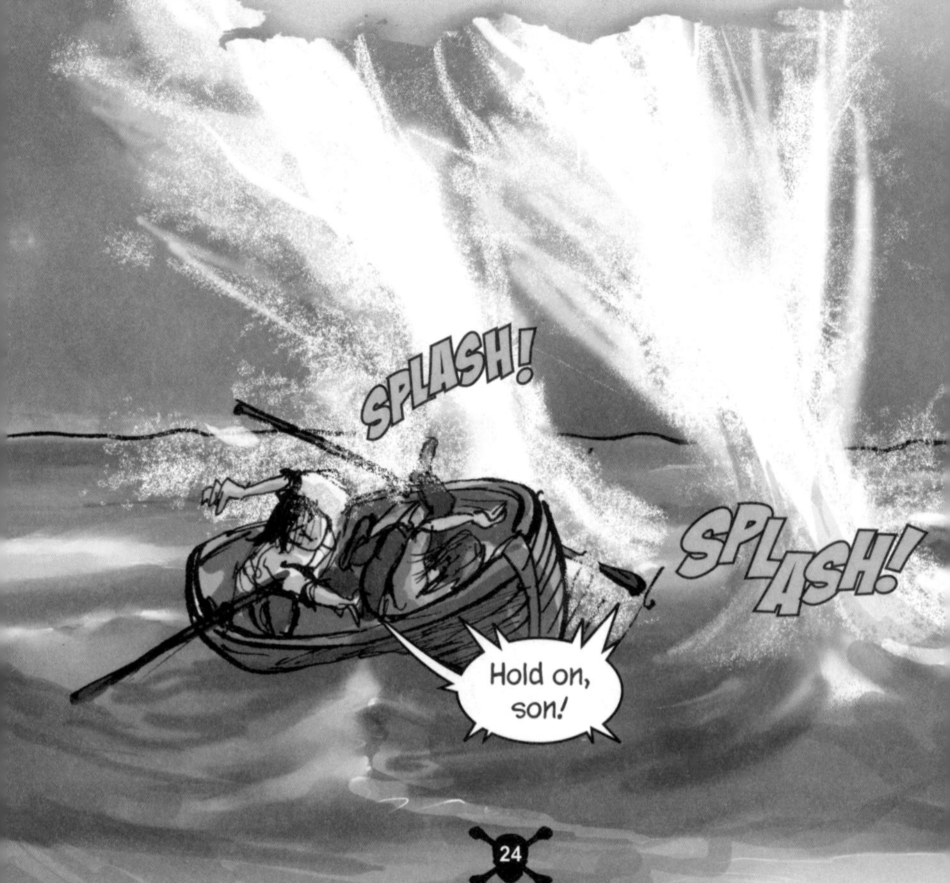
SPLASH!
SPLASH!
Hold on, son!

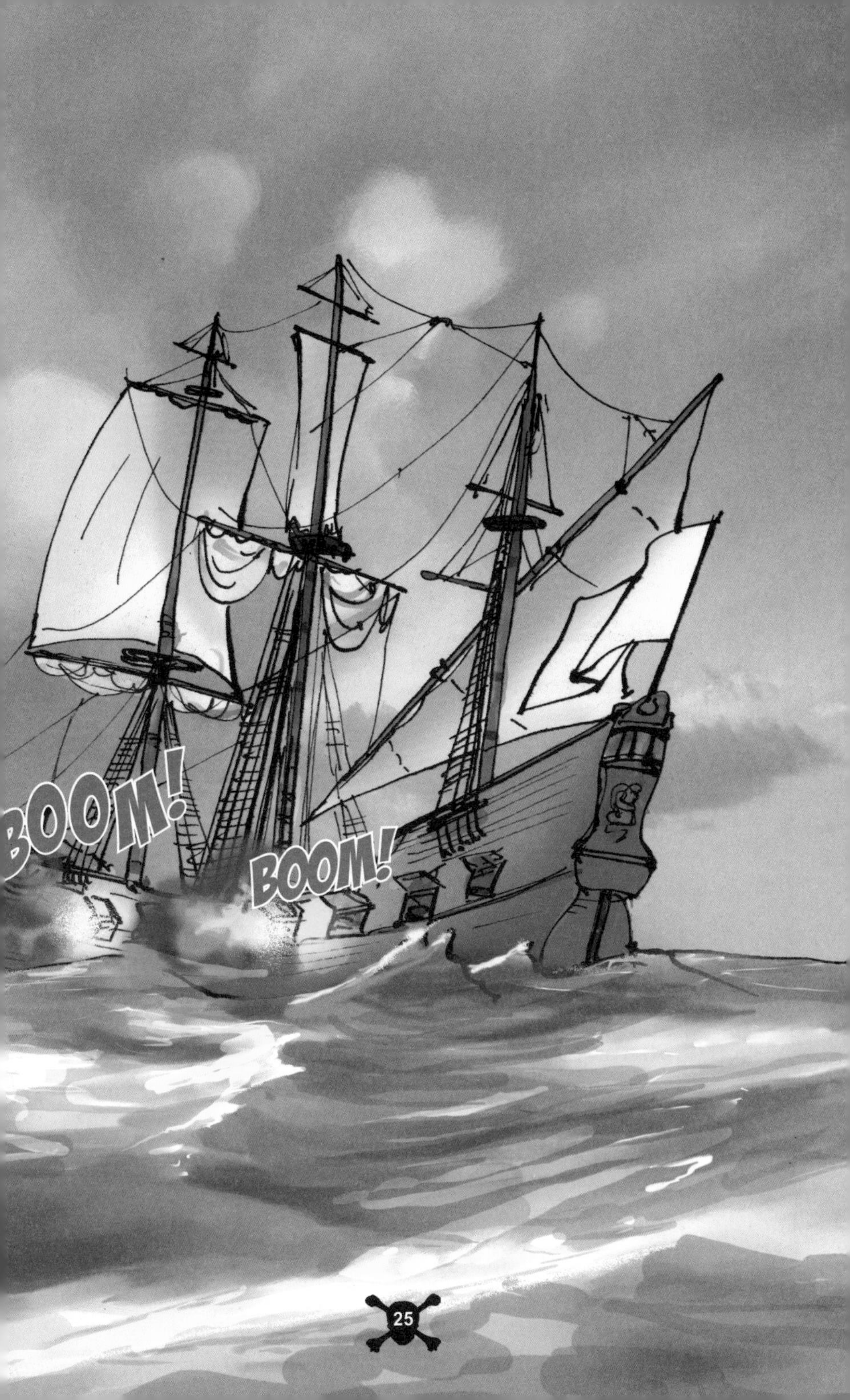
BOOM!
BOOM!

Luck was with us in our tiny boat that morning. Blackbeard's cannonballs crashed into the water around us, leaving us wet but still alive.

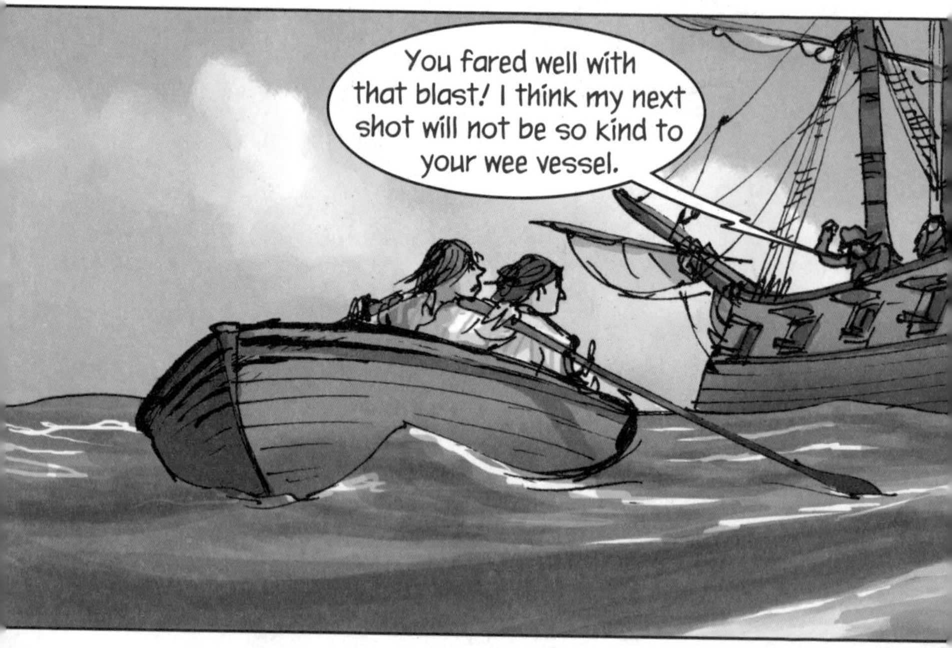
You fared well with that blast! I think my next shot will not be so kind to your wee vessel.

Blackbeard's booming laugh echoed across the water. My arms ached with rowing and my spine tingled with fear. How could I have thought Blackbeard a hero?

I looked back at the *Adventure* and saw an evil flag waving in the cold wind.

Amanda was right. Blackbeard was a bully and a mad man.

Back on the *Jane*, my father didn't tell anyone that I lied about the depth of the water. He blamed the low tide.

Soon, the tide would come in and make the waters deep enough to free the ships.

I stood at the gunwale, the ship's edge, and watched huge splashes a few yards away from us.

Each splash marked where one of Blackbeard's cannon balls landed.

They had barely missed us. Our ships were too far apart for cannonballs, but words carried easily over the water.

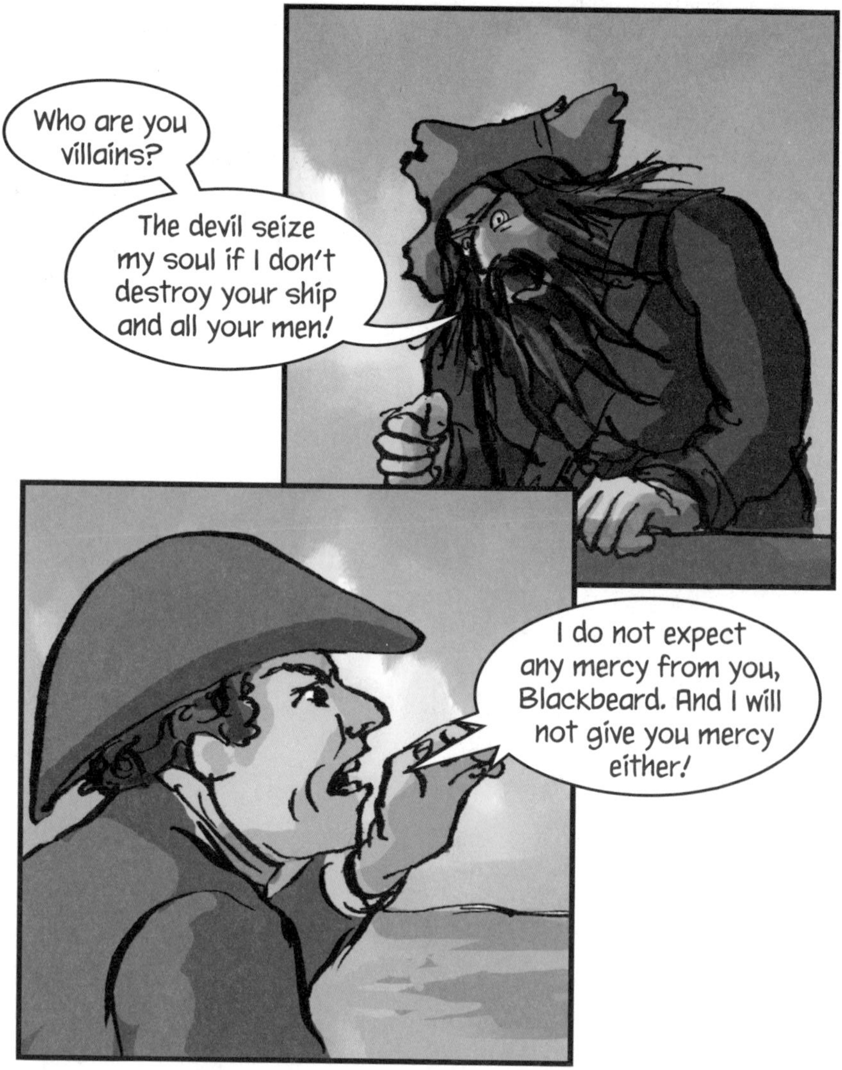
Who are you villains?
The devil seize my soul if I don't destroy your ship and all your men!
I do not expect any mercy from you, Blackbeard. And I will not give you mercy either!

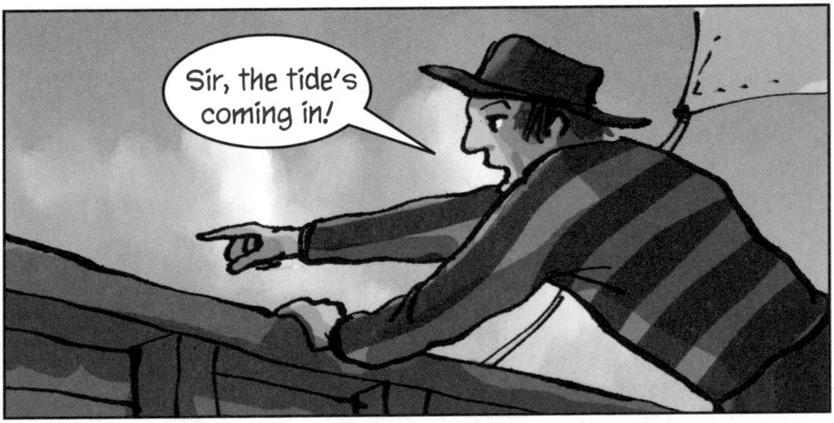
Sir, the tide's coming in!

Suddenly, both the *Jane* and the *Adventure* pulled free of the sandbanks and floated on the water once again. The tide had crept in and now the real battle would begin.

The sails of the *Adventure* puffed with wind and the ship easily turned her side to us. That could mean only one thing.

"Brace yourselves," Cameron yelled to the crew. "They're going to fire!"

A series of thunderous booms burst from the *Adventure*. Cannonballs sailed through the air.

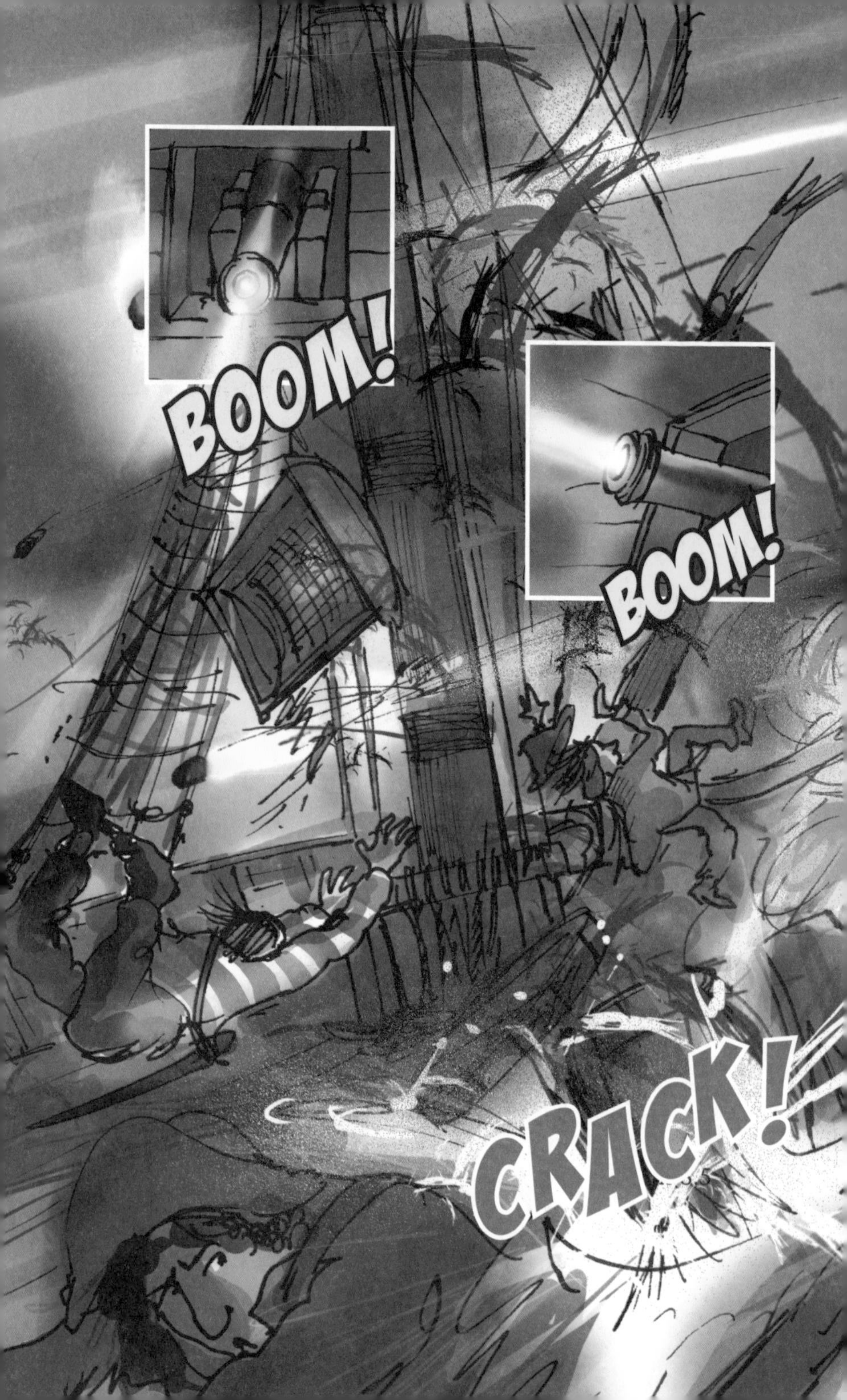
BOOM!
BOOM!
CRACK!

Chapter 5
CHAOS ABOARD THE JANE

My world exploded in a burst of gunpowder, dust, and a thousand splinters of wood.

I found myself on my back. Broken planks of wood covered my body. Carefully, I crawled out of the wreckage. I could hear sailors coughing and moaning around me.

Do not ask me how, but for the second time that day I survived when I should have perished.

My father had stood beside me, but now he was gone. Somewhere through the chaos, I heard the shouts of the crew.

I made my way to their voices.

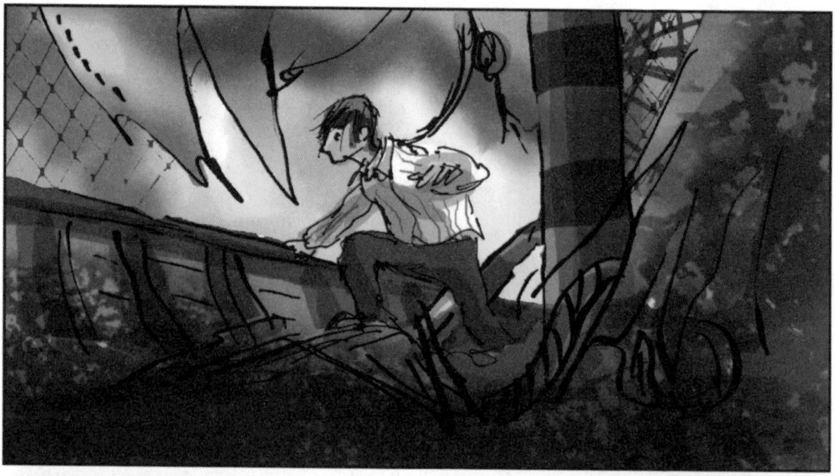

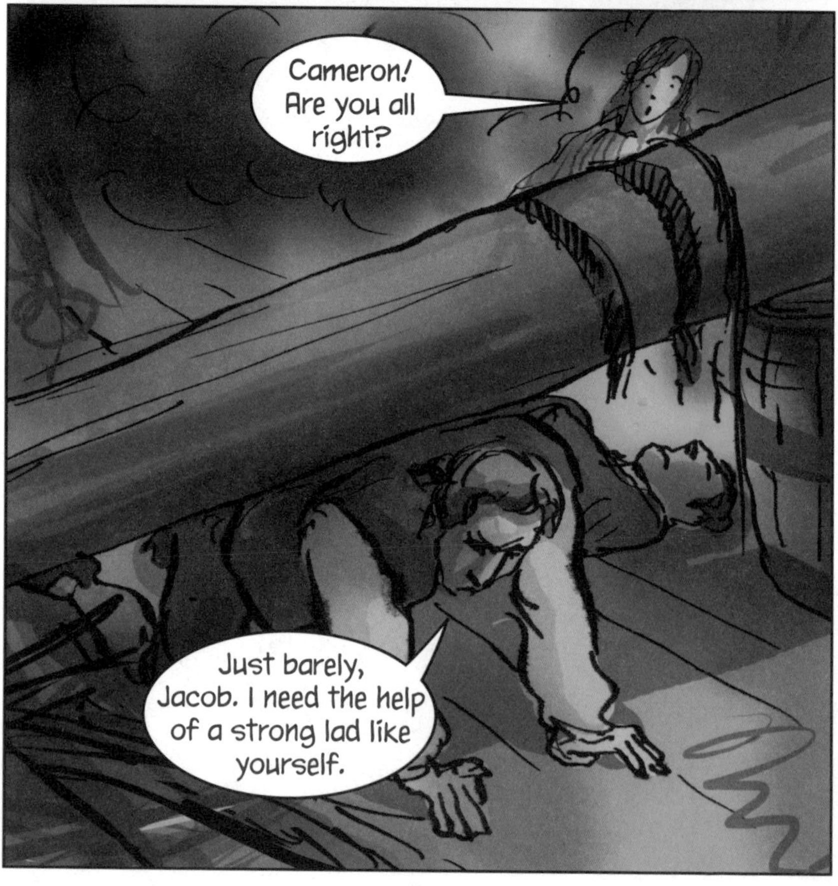
Cameron! Are you all right?
Just barely, Jacob. I need the help of a strong lad like yourself.

Cameron was the ship's quartermaster and the strongest man on board. But even he strained under the weight of the heavy beam across his back.

Cameron was holding the beam up by himself, but two other lives depended on his strength. Beneath him lay two bodies. If his strength gave out, the two men would be crushed.

It took me a moment to recognize one of the men trapped under Cameron. It was Lieutenant Maynard. His head was bleeding and he didn't look like a commander of a ship.

He smiled weakly when he saw me.

The man beside Lieutenant Maynard was unconscious, but I recognized him instantly.

"Father!"

"Aye, it's him," Cameron said through gritted teeth. "Now, be a good lad. Bring me that barrel from over there, so we can try to slip free."

I ran over to the barrel and tipped it over. Then I rolled it across the deck toward the men.

Cameron was sweating under his heavy burden. I quickly wedged the barrel under the great beam.

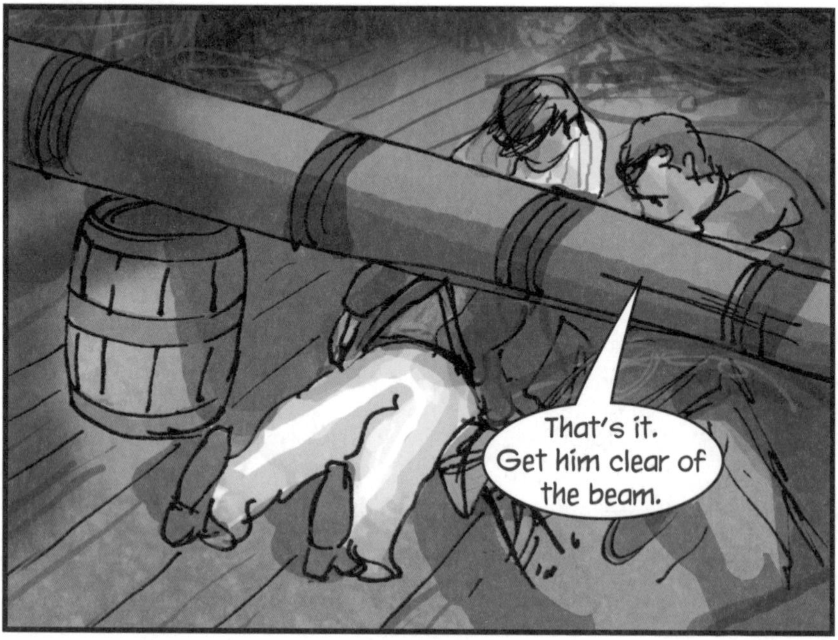
That's it.
Get him clear of
the beam.

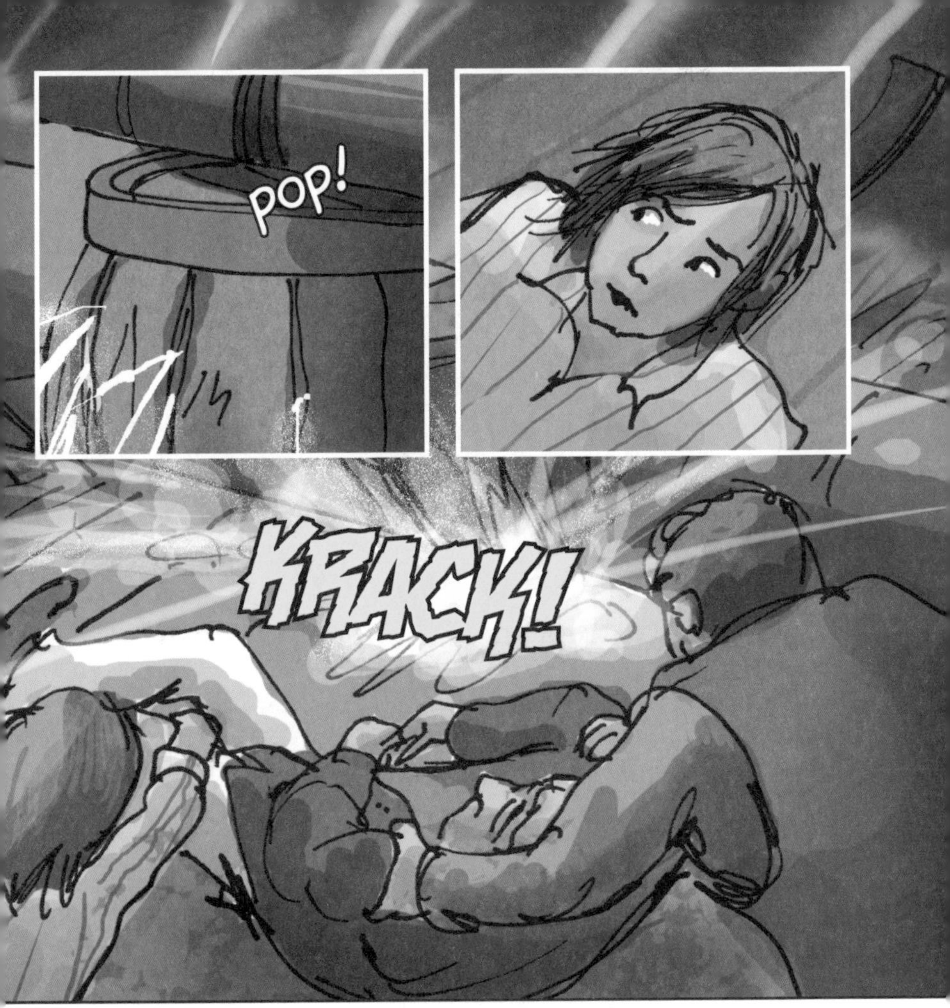
POP!
KRACK!

"Stand back!" yelled Cameron.

He leaped forward, pushing me out of the way, just as the heavy beam crushed the barrel and hit the deck with a loud thud.

"You're safe, Father," I said.

"Not quite," said Cameron.

"Look! Blackbeard approaches, Lieutenant Maynard." Cameron looked out across the water as we dragged my father to safety. "Our ship is burning and the men are panicking. He'll take us easily like this, sir."

Through the smoke, I could see the image of a white skeleton stabbing a blood red heart. It was Blackbeard's flag. He was less than a ship's length away.

"Let him come." Maynard leaned against the gunwale in pain. He winced with every breath. "I have a plan, but I need your aid, Jacob. Will you help us capture Blackbeard?"

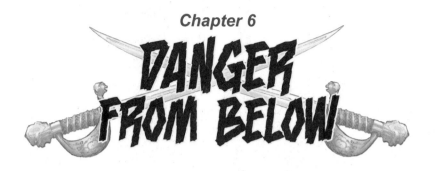

Chapter 6
DANGER FROM BELOW

A few moments later, I sat hidden behind some fallen sails, alone on the deck of the *Jane*. I tried not to panic as Blackbeard's boarding hooks grabbed our ship. I could hear the pirates as the *Adventure* came nearer.

"They have all been knocked down," yelled the pirates. "Board the ship and cut them to pieces!"

The pirates pulled the two ships together. One by one they boarded the *Jane*. Each pirate looked more cruel than the one before. But they all looked peaceful as school teachers next to their captain, Blackbeard.

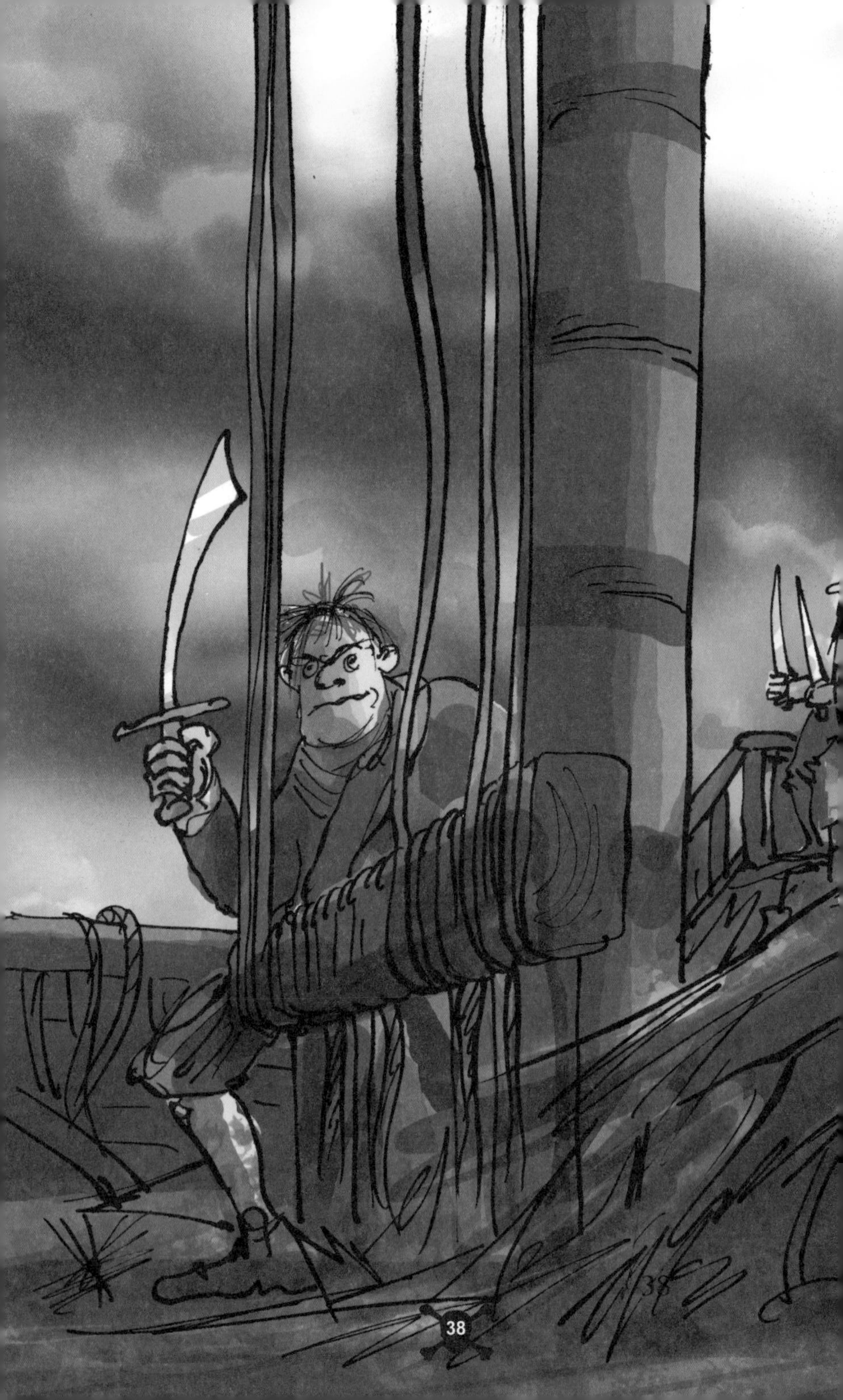

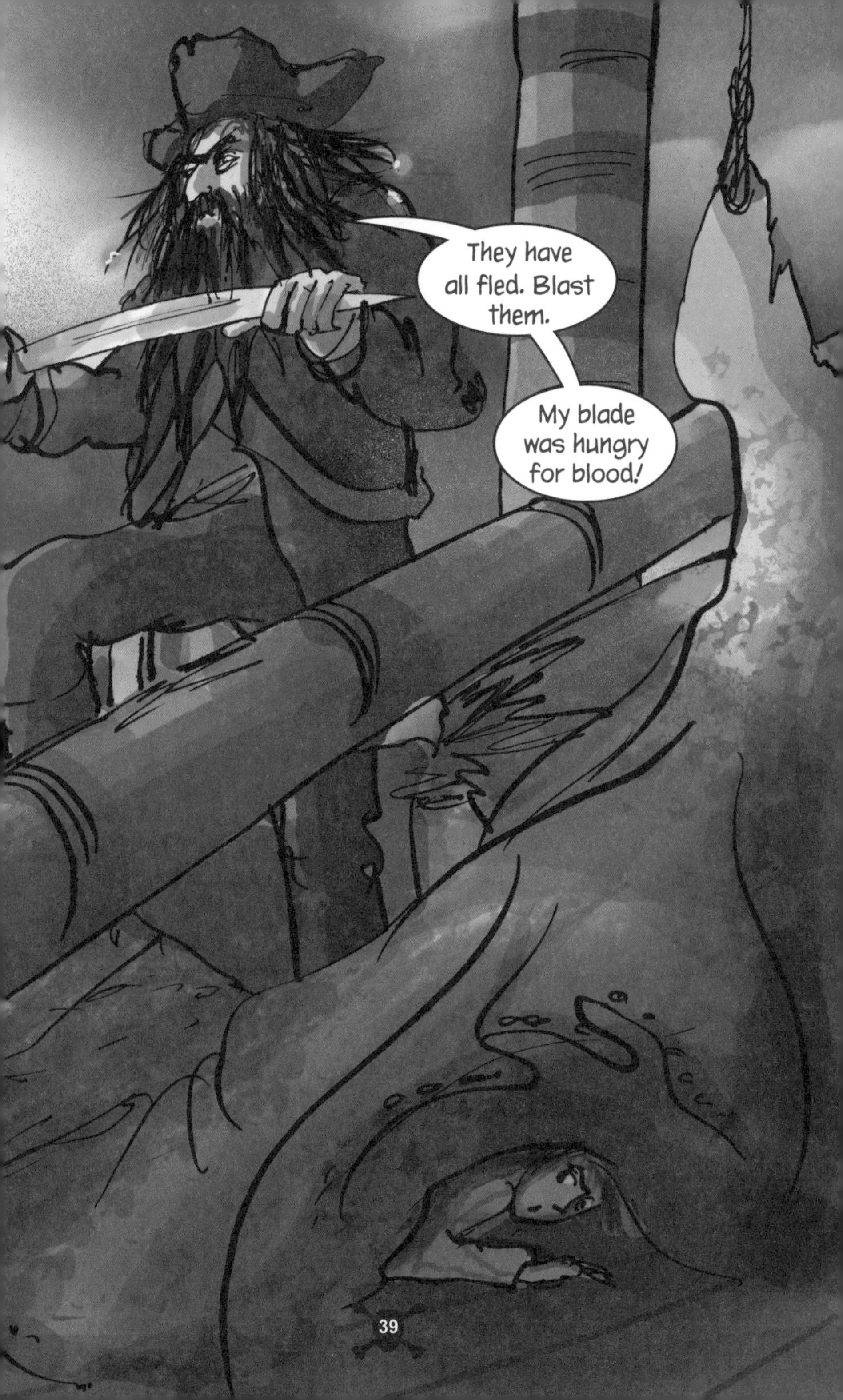
They have all fled. Blast them.
My blade was hungry for blood!

Your blade will stay hungry, Blackbeard, I thought to myself.

The pirates were swarming all over the deck, looking for survivors among our fallen sailors. They did not think to look under the sails for one small boy.

I crawled over to the hatch that led below deck. I took a deep breath.

"Now!" I yelled.

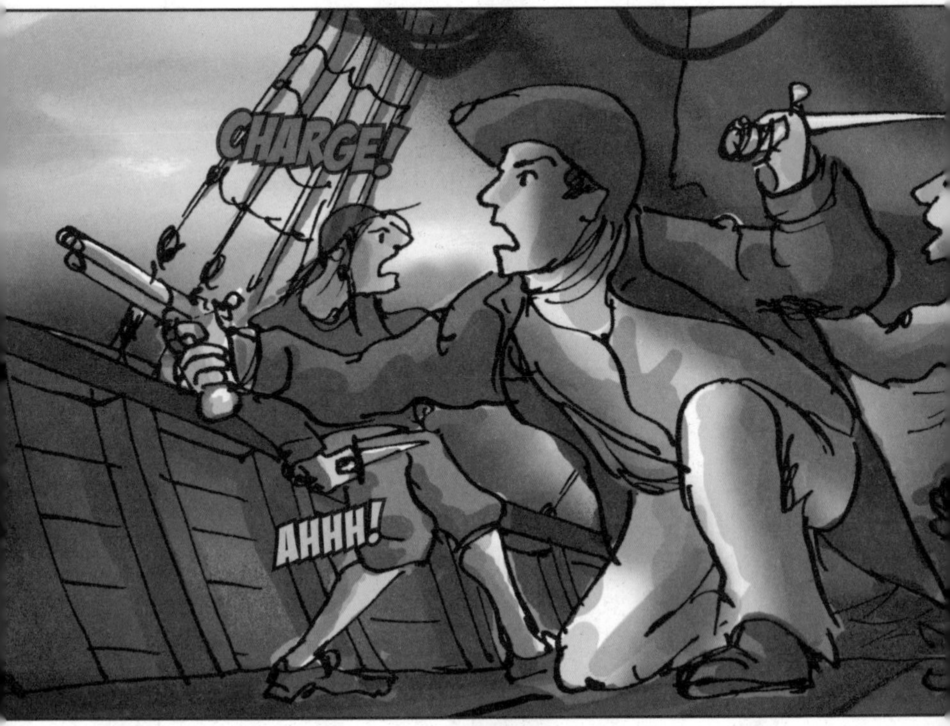
CHARGE!
AHHH!

With Lieutenant Maynard's men hidden below, Blackbeard and his pirates were caught off guard. The pirates fell under the swords of Maynard and his men. Blackbeard suffered many terrible cuts, but refused to give up. Like a monster from the sea, he lashed out at all before him. Even Lieutenant Maynard could not defeat the pirate captain.

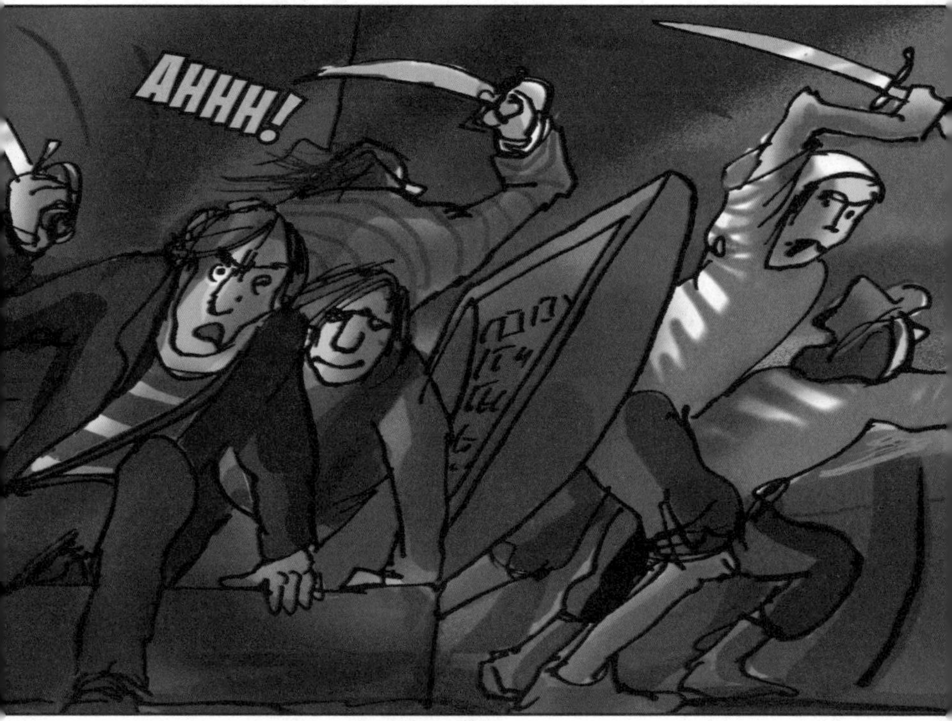
AHHH!

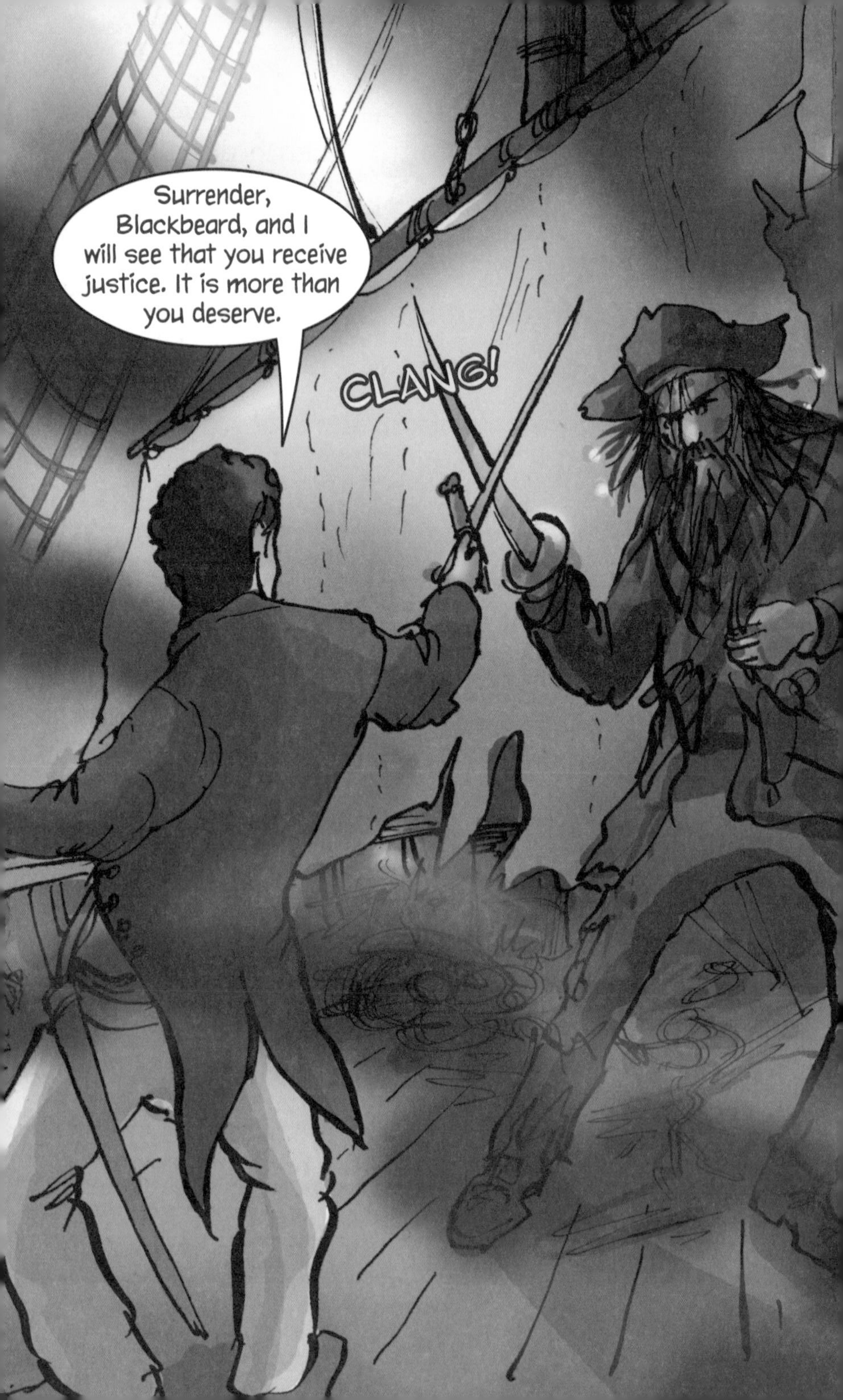
Surrender, Blackbeard, and I will see that you receive justice. It is more than you deserve.
CLANG!

Blackbeard raised his sword. It flashed in the sunlight as it swung through the air and came crashing down against Lieutenant Maynard's sword.

"What I deserve is your ship in my fleet," shouted Blackbeard to Maynard, "and your head on a pike!"

Blackbeard's cutlass shattered the lieutenant's sword. The metal pieces clattered to the deck.

Lieutenant Maynard stood helpless in front of the pirate king. He had no weapon. Blood still flowed from his head.

"I won't surrender to a scoundrel," said Lieutenant Maynard. He stood up straighter. Even with his wounds, he looked stronger and braver than Blackbeard.

The pirate king smiled.

Blackbeard's sword was still intact. His belt was still full of knives and pistols.

"I'd rather be a live scoundrel than a dead gentleman," said Blackbeard.

A crowd of pirates and sailors surrounded the two captains. They watched the two men as if they were two actors in a play.

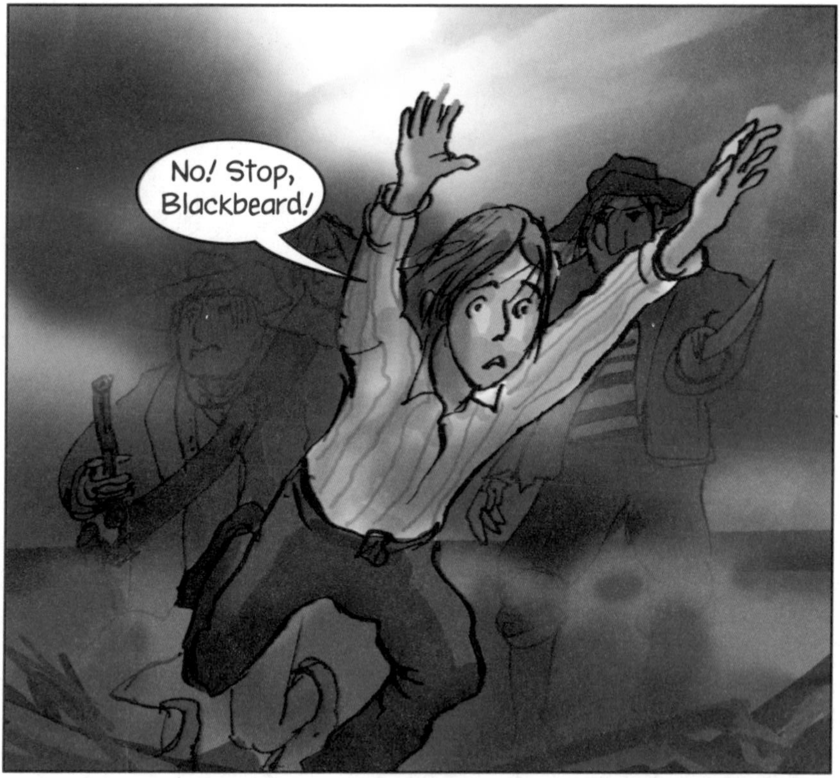
No! Stop, Blackbeard!

Blackbeard raised his sword a second time. Lieutenant Maynard raised his hands to shield his head from the coming blow.

From the crowd, Cameron appeared. His hand gripped a huge sword that he had taken from a fallen pirate.

"Blackbeard!" cried Cameron. "Only a coward strikes an unarmed man!"

Cameron swung his sword.

Flash!

Cameron didn't aim for Blackbeard's sword. Instead, his sword struck Blackbeard's neck. It neatly sliced through bone and skin, sending the pirate's head spinning across the slippery deck.

The pirates gasped.

That day, Cameron's sword proved to be stronger than Blackbeard's sword. The pirates surrendered as soon as they saw their leader die.

We sailed back to Bathtown in silence. I thought about what Amanda had asked me. Why did I think Blackbeard was so great? I didn't have an answer anymore. Instead, I thought about the men that gave their lives, so we could be free of the pirate scourge.

When our ship reached the harbor, a huge crowd gathered to meet us. A great cheer went up! They saw the bloody trophy that hung from our ship.

Blackbeard was no longer a threat. He had faced his last battle and lost.

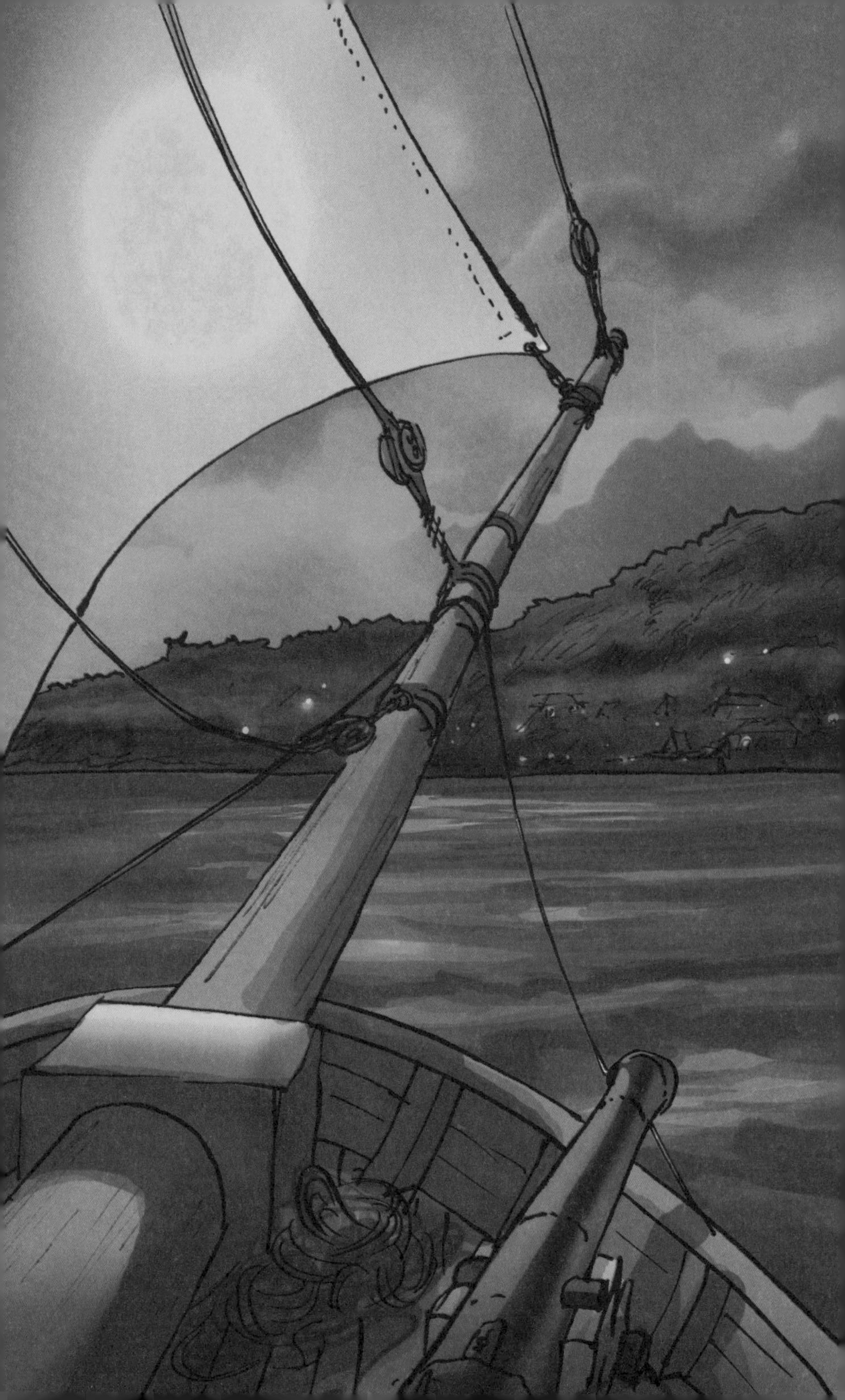

ABOUT THE AUTHOR

Liam O'Donnell was born in Northern Ireland and grew up in Canada. He's lives in Toronto, Canada and is the author of several graphic novels, including the Max Finder Mystery series of you-solve-it comics. He's never met a pirate and not sure if he ever wants to. When he's not writing stories, he loves playing video games and going camping, but not at the same time.

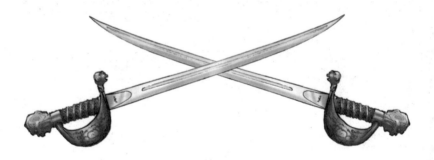

GLOSSARY

anchored (ANG-kurd)—to be secured by a heavy metal weight

braced (BRAYST)—to be prepared for a shock

cutlass (KUT-lus)—a short, curved sword

gunwale (GUN-wayl)—the upper edge of the side of a ship

hull (HUHL)—the bottom part of a ship, the part that rests partly underwater

mizzenmast (MIZ-un-mast)—the mast near the rear of the ship

perish (PAIR-ish)—to die

pike (PYK)—a sharp spear

quartermaster (KWOR-tur-mas-tur)—the member of a ship's crew who is in charge of the other crew members

sandbank (SAND-bangk)—a pile of sand in shallow water

shattered (SHAT-urd)—broken into pieces

tide (TYD)—a change in sea level caused by the pull of the sun and moon on the earth's oceans

vile (VYL)—evil or nasty

BLACKBEARD AND PIRATES

In the 1700s, there were no planes to cross the ocean, so people traveled in ships. Many ships also carried valuable cargo like rare spices or precious jewels.

Pirates were criminals who sailed the seas looking to rob ships carrying valuable cargo.

Blackbeard was one of the most feared pirates ever to sail the ocean.

Not a lot is known about Blackbeard before he became a pirate, but it is easy to see how he got his name. His face was covered with a shaggy black beard. When he went into battle, Blackbeard stuck pieces of burning rope under his hat to make it look like his beard was on fire. This scared many ship captains into giving up their cargo without a fight.

When they weren't sailing, Blackbeard and other pirates landed in the small towns on the eastern American coast to buy supplies and sell their treasure. The people in these towns quickly grew tired of the noisy and rude pirates. The people of these towns were happy when Lieutenant Maynard and his crew killed Blackbeard.

Blackbeard's death marked the end of piracy along the coast of America. Pirates continued to rob ships at sea, but since Blackbeard made his last stand in the Pamlico Sound, no other pirate attempted to set up a base on the American shore.

DISCUSSION QUESTIONS

1. Why did Jacob admire Blackbeard at the beginning of the story?

2. What happened when Jacob lied about the depth of the water the ships were sailing in?

3. What made Jacob realize that Blackbeard wasn't a hero after all? What did he think of Blackbeard after that?

4. Why did Jacob agree to stay on the deck of the ship alone when Blackbeard and his pirates stormed onboard?

WRITING PROMPTS

1. What would you do if Blackbeard and his pirates were boarding your ship? Would you prepare to fight, hide, or try to be friends with the pirates? Would you do something else? Write about it.

2. Describe the scene when Jacob and his father get off Maynard's ship and return to their town? How do their neighbors and friends react? Who is there to welcome Jacob and his father home?

3. If you were a pirate, what would your name be? What kind of ship would you sail? Write and describe your pirate life at sea. Include a map of where you might bury your treasure.

ALSO PUBLISHED BY STONE ARCH BOOKS

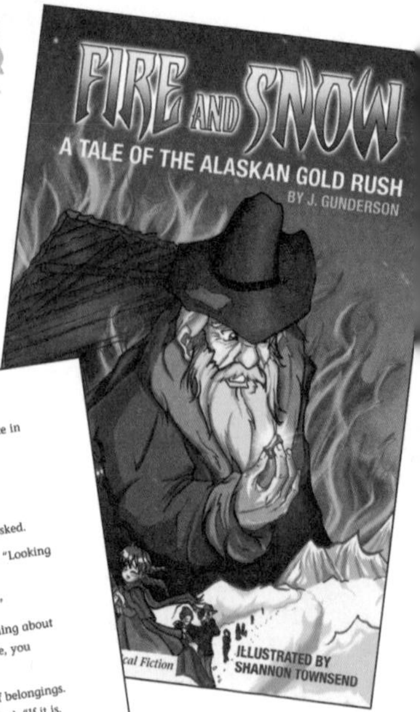

FIRE AND SNOW
A TALE OF THE ALASKAN GOLD RUSH
BY J. GUNDERSON
cal Fiction
ILLUSTRATED BY
SHANNON TOWNSEND

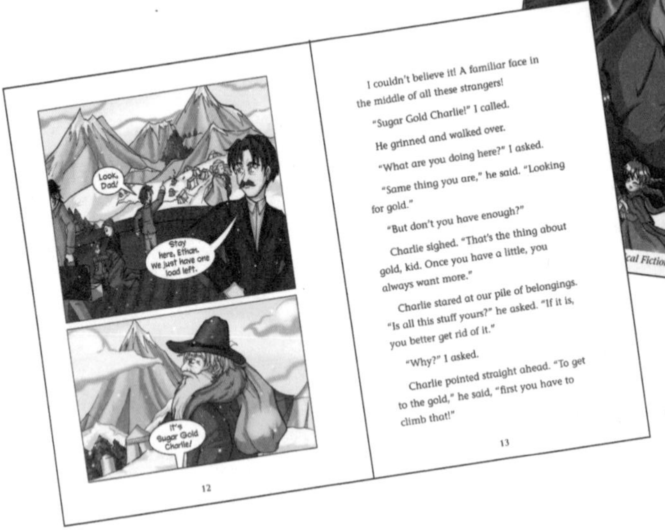

Look, Dad!
Stay here, Ethan. We just have one load left.
It's Sugar Gold Charlie!
12

I couldn't believe it! A familiar face in the middle of all these strangers!

"Sugar Gold Charlie!" I called.

He grinned and walked over.

"What are you doing here?" I asked.

"Same thing you are," he said. "Looking for gold."

"But don't you have enough?"

Charlie sighed. "That's the thing about gold, kid. Once you have a little, you always want more."

Charlie stared at our pile of belongings. "Is all this stuff yours?" he asked. "If it is, you better get rid of it."

"Why?" I asked.

Charlie pointed straight ahead. "To get to the gold," he said, "first you have to climb that!"

13

FIRE AND SNOW

A Tale of the Alaskan Gold Rush

The rivers of Alaska are flowing with gold! At least that's the story Ethan Michelson hears from excited prospectors. He and his family leave their comfortable home in Seattle to seek their fortune in the snowy North. Ethan must brave an avalanche, cross an icy river, and battle a deadly fire before he can decide if the hunt for treasure is worth the risk.

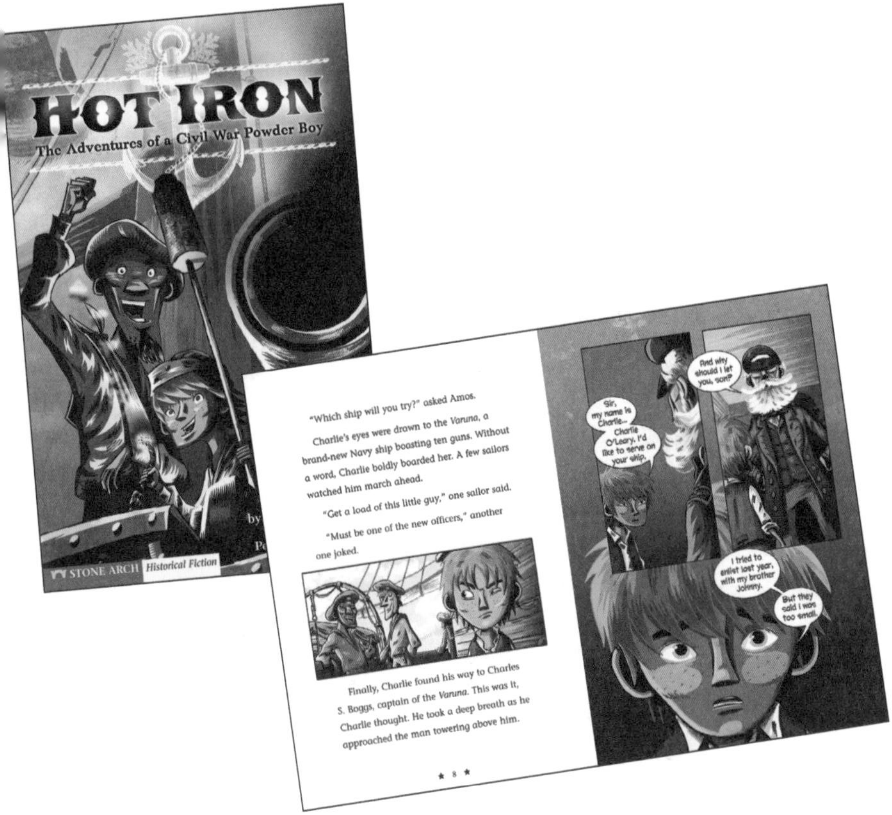
HOT IRON
The Adventures of a Civil War Powder Boy
STONE ARCH Historical Fiction

"Which ship will you try?" asked Amos.

Charlie's eyes were drawn to the *Varuna*, a brand-new Navy ship boasting ten guns. Without a word, Charlie boldly boarded her. A few sailors watched him march ahead.

"Get a load of this little guy," one sailor said.

"Must be one of the new officers," another one joked.

Finally, Charlie found his way to Charles S. Boggs, captain of the *Varuna*. This was it, Charlie thought. He took a deep breath as he approached the man towering above him.

★ 8 ★

Sir, my name is Charlie... Charlie O'Leary. I'd like to serve on your ship.
And why should I let you, son?
I tried to enlist last year, with my brother Johnny.
But they said I was too small.

HOT IRON

The Adventures of a Civil War Powder Boy

Twelve-year old Charlie O'Leary signs aboard the USS Varuna as it steams its way toward the mouth of the Mississippi River to fight the Confederate Navy. Charlie is short enough, and swift enough, to race through the crowded ship and fetch gunpowder for the big guns on deck. The cannons boom like thunder. Their hot iron shells blast through enemy ships, ripping canvas, wood, and metal. Charlie hopes to find his brother Johnny among the Varuna's fleet. But will their ships survive the awesome Battle of New Orleans?

INTERNET SITES

Do you want to know more about subjects related to this book? Or are you interested in learning about other topics? Then check out FactHound, a fun, easy way to find Internet sites.

Our investigative staff has already sniffed out great sites for you!

Here's how to use FactHound:

1. Visit *www.facthound.com*

2. Select your grade level.

3. To learn more about subjects related to this book, type in the book's ISBN number: 1598893092.

4. Click the Fetch It button.

FactHound will fetch the best Internet sites for you.